Lewis and Clark and Me

LEWIS AND CLARK AND ME

A DOG'S TALE

LAURIE MYERS

ILLUSTRATIONS BY
MICHAEL DOOLING

HENRY HOLT AND COMPANY · NEW YORK

My appreciation to the Lewis and Clark Trail Heritage Foundation for its dedication to excellence and passing on one of the greatest adventures in history. —L. M.

Many thanks to the men of the Lewis and Clark Discovery Expedition of St. Charles, Missouri, especially Peter Geery. —M. D.

NOTE TO READERS: The extracts from Meriwether Lewis's journal published in this book retain their original spelling.

———————————————

Henry Holt and Company, LLC
Publishers since 1866
115 West 18th Street, New York, New York 10011
www.henryholt.com

Henry Holt is a registered trademark of Henry Holt and Company, LLC
Text copyright © 2002 by Laurie Myers
Illustrations copyright © 2002 by Michael Dooling
All rights reserved.
Distributed in Canada by H. B. Fenn and Company Ltd.
Library of Congress Cataloging-in-Publication Data
Myers, Laurie. Lewis and Clark and me: a dog's tale /
Laurie Myers; illustrations by Michael Dooling.   p.   cm.
Includes bibliographical references.
Summary: Seaman, Meriwether Lewis's Newfoundland dog, describes Lewis and Clark's expedition,
which he accompanied from St. Louis to the Pacific Ocean. 1. Seaman (Dog)—Juvenile fiction.
2. Lewis, Meriwether, 1774–1809—Juvenile fiction. 3. Clark, William, 1770–1838—Juvenile fiction.
4. Lewis and Clark Expedition (1804–1806)—Juvenile fiction. [1. Seaman (Dog)—Fiction.
2. Lewis, Meriwether, 1774–1809—Fiction. 3. Clark, William, 1770–1838—Fiction. 4. Lewis and
Clark Expedition (1804–1806)—Fiction. 5. Dogs—Fiction. 6. Newfoundland dog—Fiction.]
I. Dooling, Michael, ill. II. Title. PZ7.M9873 Le 2002   [Fic]—dc21   00-47298
ISBN 0-8050-6368-4 / First Edition—2002 / Designed by Donna Mark
Printed in Hong Kong
1   3   5   7   9   10   8   6   4   2

The artist used oil on linen canvas to create the color illustrations for this book.

Contents

LEWIS AND CLARK AND ME

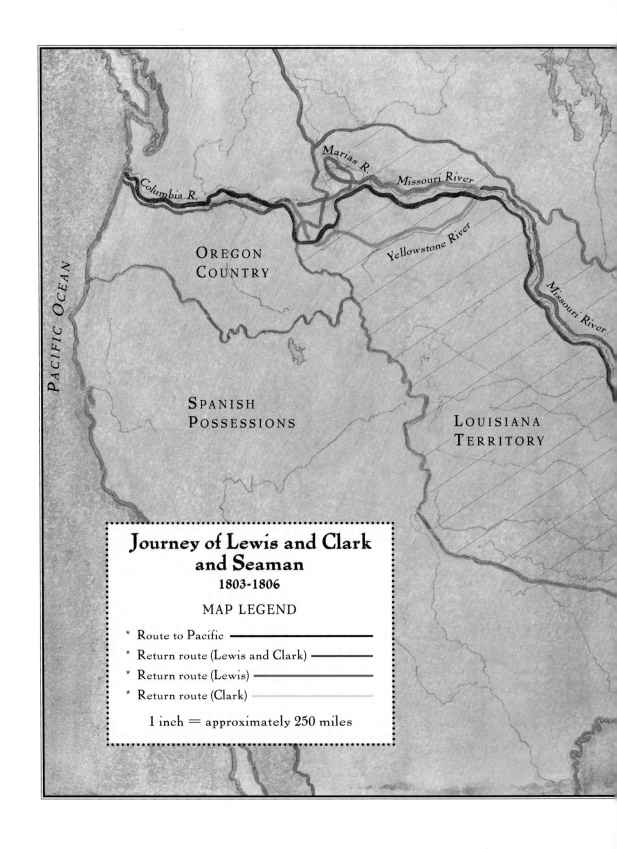

PACIFIC OCEAN

Columbia R.

Marias R.

Missouri River

Yellowstone River

Missouri River

OREGON
COUNTRY

SPANISH
POSSESSIONS

LOUISIANA
TERRITORY

Journey of Lewis and Clark and Seaman
1803-1806

MAP LEGEND

* Route to Pacific ———————
* Return route (Lewis and Clark) ———
* Return route (Lewis) ——————
* Return route (Clark) ··············

1 inch = approximately 250 miles

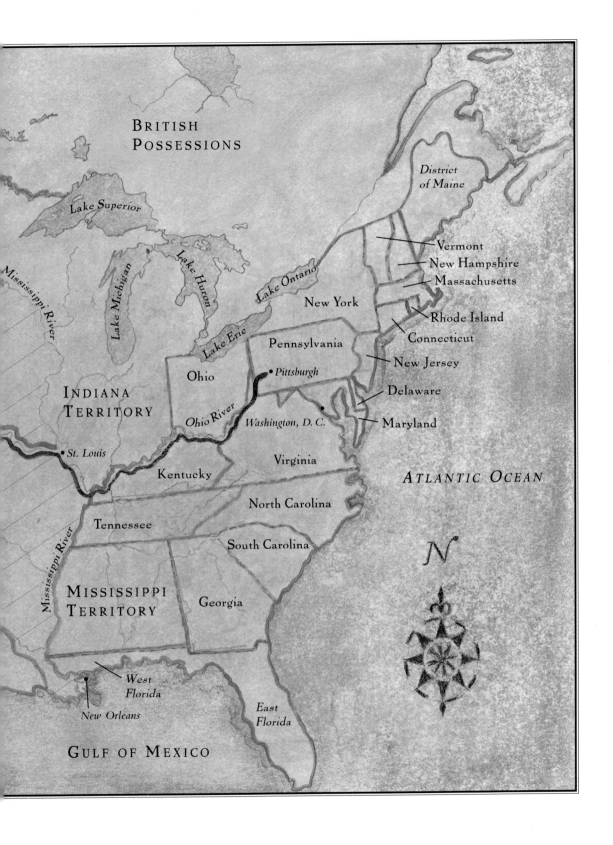

BRITISH
POSSESSIONS

Lake Superior

Lake Michigan

Lake Huron

Lake Ontario

Lake Erie

Mississippi River

*District
of Maine*

Vermont
New Hampshire
Massachusetts

New York

Rhode Island
Connecticut

Pennsylvania

• *Pittsburgh*

New Jersey

Ohio

Delaware

INDIANA
TERRITORY

Ohio River

Washington, D. C.

Maryland

• *St. Louis*

Virginia

Kentucky

ATLANTIC OCEAN

North Carolina

Tennessee

South Carolina

Mississippi River

MISSISSIPPI
TERRITORY

Georgia

N

*West
Florida*

*East
Florida*

New Orleans

GULF OF MEXICO

INTRODUCTION

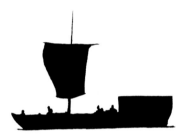

When Thomas Jefferson was a boy, one of his teachers inspired him to learn more about the West, that vast territory stretching from the Mississippi River to the Pacific Ocean. Years later, after Thomas Jefferson became president of the United States in 1801, Spain, France, and England were also interested in controlling this area.

Spain already owned New Orleans and the Louisiana Territory, which was a large portion of the West. In 1800, the French, under Napoleon, signed a secret treaty giving the Spanish territory to France. At the same time, the British, who had an active fur trade in Canada, were exploring farther south to find a water route to the Pacific Ocean to increase their trade. Whoever controlled that water passageway would control trade. When Thomas Jefferson learned of all these activities, he purchased the Louisiana Territory and quickly planned his own expedition to find a water passageway to the Pacific Ocean. In 1803 Congress voted to provide the money for the expedition.

Thomas Jefferson needed an extraordinary man to lead such an important trip. He chose the man he trusted most, his personal secretary and friend, Meriwether Lewis. Lewis was perfect for the position. He had grown up in the Appalachian Mountains, was an expert hunter, and had a keen mind.

Lewis invited William Clark to join him on the expedition. Lewis had served briefly under Clark in the army and greatly respected him. Together the two military captains led one of the most exciting journeys of exploration in American history. They spent two and a half years traveling seven thousand miles to the Pacific Ocean and back.

Meriwether Lewis's faithful and courageous dog, Seaman, accompanied the thirty-three-member expedition. He acted as hunter, retriever, guard dog, and peacemaker with the Indians. At times he risked his life to protect the men.

Seaman shared the joy as well as the suffering with the expedition members. He delighted in a good meal and an evening of entertainment by the campfire. And he suffered hunger, pain, cold, and the torment of gnats and mosquitoes.

Several of the men kept journals during the trip. Early in the expedition the journals refer to Seaman as "Captain Lewis's dog." By the end, they routinely use "our dog." Seaman's perseverance and faithfulness made him an important and beloved member of the expedition. This is Seaman's story.

ONE

THE BEGINNING

Sometimes in my dreams, Lewis and I and the Mandan Indians are chasing buffalo across snow-covered plains. The smell of buffalo fills my nostrils, and the rumble of the herd echoes in my ears.

Sometimes George Drouillard, our best hunter, only wounds a deer that is swimming across the river and I swim out to retrieve it. The deer tries to get away, but I am much too strong and too good a swimmer. The men cheer me on from the banks.

Sometimes it's just Lewis and me. We stand by the Great Falls, the spray from the water misting our faces. We walk along the sandy beaches of the Pacific Ocean for the first time. Or it is just a typical day when Lewis and I hike through the woods together, while Clark and the men row or sail the boats on the river.

My dreams are more vivid than life itself. Everything is brighter, clearer. The smell of the woods is richer. The desperation of the prey is keener. The victory sweeter.

Sometimes when I'm dreaming, a well-meaning person sees my nose twitch or my legs jerk.

"Okay, boy. It's just a dream," they say, and pat my shoulder.

Just a dream.

They say it as though it were some small and insignificant experience, not worthy of attention. They don't understand. I love my dreams. I don't want them to end. They take me back to a place I was made for . . . back to a place that makes me alive . . . the most beautiful place in the world . . . the wilderness.

"Seaman!"

I glance at the man beside me.

"Look alive. Here's buyers."

Something caught my attention beyond him, down the wharf—a group of men, but I saw only one. It was Lewis. He was a full head taller than the other men I had known on the docks. And he was dressed in a different way—white breeches and a short blue coat with buttons that shone in the sun. A tall pointed hat with a feather made him look even taller.

Lewis walked along the dock with a large stride. There was a purpose about him. My life on the wharves was good, but I was a young dog and yearned for more. At the time I didn't know exactly what. I sensed that this man was part of what I wanted. I sat straighter as he approached. The man who owned me stood straighter, too. Lewis slowed.

"Need a dog, sir?" my man asked.

"I'm lookin'," Lewis replied. He stooped down and looked me right in the eye. I wagged my tail and stepped forward. I wanted to sniff this strange man. He extended his hand for me. He didn't smell like any I had ever smelled, and it made me want to sniff him all over.

Lewis scratched the back of my neck, where I liked to be scratched.

"I'm headed out west, up the Missouri River," Lewis said.

My man's face brightened.

"This dog be perfect, sir. These dogs can swim. Newfoundlands, they call them. Rescue a drowning man in rough water or in a storm. Look at these paws. You won't find another dog with paws like that. They's webbed." He spread my toes to show the webbing.

"So they are," Lewis replied. Lewis began feeling my chest and hindquarters. His hands were large and muscular.

"Water rolls off this coat," my man added. He pulled up a handful of my thick, dense double coat.

Lewis examined my coat and nodded.

"I know the Mississippi, sir, but I don't know the Meesori," my man said.

"It's off the Mississippi, headin' northwest."

"North, you say. Ah. It'll be cold up that river.

Won't bother this one, though." He patted me firmly on the back.

Lewis stood and looked around. He found a piece of wood that had broken off a crate. He showed it to me, then threw it.

"Go," he said.

I wanted to go. I wanted to do whatever this man asked. But I belonged to another. I looked at my man.

"Go on," he said.

I ran for the stick and returned it to Lewis.

"How much?" Lewis asked.

"Twenty dollars. And a bargain at that."

Lewis looked down at me. I lifted my head proudly.

"Won't find a better dog than this. Perfect for your trip," my man said, trying to convince Lewis.

It wasn't necessary. Lewis wanted me. I could tell. He had liked me the minute he saw me. The feeling was mutual. Lewis paid my man twenty dollars.

"Does he have a name?" Lewis asked.

"I been callin' him Seaman, but you can name him anything you like."

"Come, Seaman," Lewis called.

As we walked away, my rope in his hand, he put his other hand on my head. After that, he didn't need a rope. I would follow this man to the ends of the earth.

———————

. . . the dog was of the newfoundland breed one that I prised much for his docility and qualifications generally for my journey. . . .

Meriwether Lewis
November 16, 1803

TWO

SQUIRRELS

I caught fish off the docks. I chased animals in the woods. But hunting came alive for me on the river—the Ohio, Lewis called it.

I have always loved the water, so the day we boarded the boat and pushed out onto the Ohio River was just about the happiest day of my life. Lewis was excited, too. I could tell by the way he walked. And his voice was louder than usual.

The men were also excited. I could hear it in their voices. They didn't complain when they loaded the boat. Lewis was telling them what to load and how to load it. Anyway, that afternoon,

Lewis and I and some men started down the river.

I rode in the back of the boat. It was the highest place and gave me the best view. From there I could scan both banks and the water with just a glance. The first two weeks I couldn't get enough of it. There were animals I had not seen before. Smells I had not smelled. My skin tingled with excitement.

The river was low, and the men had to pole much of the way. When they weren't poling, they were digging channels for our boat or hiring oxen to pull the boat from the shore.

We were only a couple of weeks down the river when I had my first great day of hunting. The river wasn't quite as shallow and the current not too strong, so the crew rowed along leisurely.

I was lying on the back deck of the boat. I had just scanned the shore—nothing of interest, just a few beaver and a deer. I decided to close my eyes for a nap. I blinked a few times and was ready to lay my head on my paws when something on the water up ahead caught my eye. I stuck my nose in the air and sniffed. I recognized the scent immediately. Squirrel.

A squirrel on water? That was unusual. I had seen plenty of squirrels, but I had never seen one swim. There was something else strange. The smell of squirrel was especially strong. I had never known one squirrel to project so powerful a scent.

I stood to take a look. Right away I spotted a squirrel off the starboard side. He was swimming across the river. Another squirrel followed close behind. Without a second thought, I leaned over the side of the boat to get a better look.

I saw another squirrel. And another. I could not believe my eyes; hundreds of squirrels were crossing the river. The water up ahead was almost black with them. Every muscle in my body tightened to full alert.

Lewis was on the other side of the boat, talking to two of the men. I turned to him and barked.

"What is it?" he asked.

It is impossible to describe the urge I felt. It was as strong as anything I had ever known. I had to get those squirrels.

I barked again. Lewis scanned the water ahead.

"Look at that," he said to the men. "Squirrels crossing the river. Now why would they do that?"

"Food?" one man suggested.

Lewis paused for a moment. "There are hickory nuts on both banks."

"Migrating?" suggested the other.

Lewis nodded. "Maybe. Or perhaps they're—"

I barked again. They were wasting time wondering why the squirrels were crossing. It didn't matter. The squirrels were there. Hundreds of them, right in front of us. Sometimes men spend too much time thinking. They miss the fun of life.

"They'd make a fine supper," the first man suggested with a smile.

Lewis nodded. He looked at me. "Let's see what you can do, Seaman. Go on. Fetch us a squirrel."

That's what I was waiting for. I sprang off the boat and hit the water swimming. I was going to get every squirrel in that river for Lewis. My webbed feet made it easy. I reached the first squirrel in just minutes.

When it saw me, its eyes bulged with fear. It tried to steer its sleek, fat body away. In one swift move I grabbed it by the neck and killed it. I carried it back to the boat. Lewis leaned over the side and took it from me.

"Good dog. Fetch another," he said.

The crew had stopped rowing, and the boat drifted slowly toward the mass of squirrels.

"Look at Captain Lewis's dog!" yelled one of the rowers.

I turned and started swimming again. I could hear the men cheering me on. In two strokes I was on another squirrel.

"Good dog!" Lewis yelled. "Go!"

"Go," the crew echoed. "Go, Seaman, go!"

I went. And went. Over and over, I went. I went until I was exhausted. I don't know how long it lasted. Maybe one hour. Maybe four.

All I know is that when I finished, there was a pile of squirrels in the boat. Lewis and the crew were laughing and cheering. All the rest of the day the men were patting me and saying, "Good dog" and "Good boy" and "We'll be eatin' good tonight." The admiration of the crew was great, but the look of pride on Lewis's face was better than all the men's praise added together.

That night the men fried the squirrels, and we ate well.

In the three years that followed, I hunted almost every day. But the squirrels on the Ohio were my favorite.

———————

. . . observed a number of squirrels swiming the Ohio . . . they appear to be making to the south; . . . I made my dog take as many each day as I had occation for, they wer fat and I thought them when fryed a pleasent food . . . he would take the squirel in the water kill them and swiming bring them in his mouth to the boat. . . .

Meriwether Lewis
September 11, 1803

THREE

— · —————————— · —

BEAR-DOG

"Indians."

We had not been on the shore very long before I heard Lewis say the word.

Lewis and Clark and I had crossed the river to make some observations. That's when these Indians appeared. They were different from other people I had known—the boatmen and city folk. These people smelled of animal skins and smoke and a hint of dried blood.

I didn't sense that Lewis or Clark were concerned, so I wasn't. The Indians seemed friendly enough.

Lewis talked to them. It wasn't until later that I realized Lewis gave the same talk to every group of Indians we met. He talked about the "great white father" in Washington.

The Indians listened patiently as one of the English-speaking Indians translated. Lewis used hand motions to help. As he talked on, it became obvious to me that the Indians were not interested in Lewis or what he was saying. They were staring at me. Finally, Lewis realized what was going on, and he invited the Indians to take a closer look.

They gathered around. They touched me. They whispered about me. They acted like they had never seen a dog before. Then I noticed an Indian dog standing to the side. I took one look at that animal and realized why they were so interested in me.

That dog could not have been more than twenty pounds. Newfoundlands can weigh up to 150 pounds, and I'm a large Newfoundland. If that scrawny dog was the only dog they had seen, then I was a strange sight indeed.

"Bear," one of the English-speaking Indians said.

I looked up. He was pointing at me.

"Dog," Lewis replied patiently.

The Indian looked at his own dog. He looked back at me.

"Bear," he said again.

Lewis looked at me and smiled. Clark was smiling, too. I lifted my head.

"I guess he does look like a bear," Lewis said.

Lewis picked up a stick and threw it.

"Fetch," he said.

I fetched.

"Stay," he said.

I stayed.

"Sit," he said.

I sat.

The Indians were impressed.

"Dog," Lewis said politely. Lewis was always nice.

The Indian who had called me "bear" turned to consult with his friends.

Finally, he turned.

"Bear-dog," he said with satisfaction.

Lewis smiled.

"Yes, I guess you could call him bear-dog."

Later, George Drouillard explained to us that the

Indians don't have a separate word for *horse*. They call a horse "elk-dog." I guess it made sense for them to call me a bear-dog.

The Indian suddenly turned and walked through the crowd to his horse. He pulled out three beaver skins. He held them out to Lewis.

"For bear-dog," he said.

It wasn't often that I saw Lewis surprised. He was then.

I took a step closer to Lewis.

Lewis looked the Indian square in the eye and said, "No trade. Bear-dog special."

As we rode back to camp in the boat, Lewis said to me, "Three beaver skins! Can you believe that?"

No, I could not. The idea that Lewis and I would ever separate was unthinkable. Not many dogs and men fit together like Lewis and I. If you have ever experienced it, then you know what I'm talking about. And if you haven't, well, it's hard to explain. All I can tell you is that when a dog and a man fit like Lewis and I did, nothing can separate them. Lewis said it best.

"No trade."

. . . one of the Shawnees a respectable looking Indian offered me three beverskins for my dog with which he appeared much pleased . . . of course there was no bargan, I had given 20$ for this dogg myself—

Meriwether Lewis
November 16, 1803

FOUR

BUFFALO CALF

Lewis and I loved to walk. We spent hours on shore, while the men rowed or sailed the boats in the river. It was on one of these walks that a buffalo calf began following Lewis.

Lewis and I had stopped by the river's edge to survey the flow of the water when the calf wandered up. I do not know what it was thinking. Probably nothing. I've never considered buffaloes to be smart. And they are nearsighted. That's how the Indians chase them off those cliffs. Anyway, this buffalo calf took one look at me and went straight to Lewis.

When Lewis walked on, the calf followed, right on his heels. That calf was acting as though Lewis were his mother.

Now, when Lewis and I walked, we sometimes split up. I'd hear an animal, or smell something that I needed to check out, and I would head in a different direction. Not this time. I stayed with Lewis and the calf, but I walked a few yards behind. The calf kept looking back at me. Maybe he was hoping I would disappear so that he could have Lewis all to himself, or something ridiculous like that.

Lewis stopped by the river again. The calf stayed by his side. I stared at the calf. Why was he attaching himself to Lewis? Did he think he was going to stay with Lewis permanently?

I needed to scare off the calf. That would put an end to this nonsense. I was sure Lewis didn't want him around any more than I did. I decided a growl would be enough. After all, this was just a calf. Of course, buffaloes are stubborn. If I needed to, I could throw my paws into the air and play the part of bear–dog. That would work.

I took a deep breath in and started a low growl. It was not my most vicious growl, just a low, constant rumble to let that calf know he wasn't welcome. The calf looked over his shoulder at me, then took a step closer to Lewis. That didn't make any sense. Lewis and I were a team; moving close to Lewis was like moving close to me.

Next, Lewis did something that surprised me. He reached out his hand and placed it on the calf's head, the same way he put his hand on my head sometimes. That was the last thing I expected. Could it be that Lewis wanted the calf to stay with us? What was Lewis thinking?

"Where's your mother?" Lewis said.

At that moment everything became clear, like the streams in the mountains. I looked at the calf's eyes. He didn't have those piercing black eyes that the adult buffaloes have when they're mad. His eyes were soft, tinted with fear.

The calf was afraid of me. How could I have missed that? The calf reeked of fear. He was twice my size, but he was frightened nonetheless. I backed away.

Lewis scratched the calf's ears. I was touched by the gentle way Lewis handled him. It reminded me of the way Lewis handled a sick Hidatsa Indian boy one winter. The boy's mother had brought him to Lewis for treatment, and the boy was very frightened. I could smell it. Lewis treated him gently, and the boy's fear left.

Lewis turned and started back toward the boat, the buffalo calf close at his heels. I followed, keeping my distance so as not to scare the calf. When we arrived at the boat, Lewis and I got in. The calf watched us from the shore as we pulled away.

Suddenly it all seemed very funny to me. Imagine a buffalo calf thinking it could be a part of our lives. How in the world would he get in and out of the boat? I thought about the ridiculous sight. It's times like that when I wish I could laugh. I wagged my tail.

Now, when I think back on the whole situation, I guess I was jealous. I see that in young dogs. A new puppy comes along, all playful and cunning, and everyone pats it and plays with it. Then the big dogs jump all over themselves trying to get noticed.

Well, I didn't jump all over myself, but I suppose that if it had gone much further, I might have. My feelings for Lewis have always run strong.

———————

. . . walking on shore this evening I met with a buffaloe calf which attatched itself to me and continued to follow close at my heels untill I embarked and left it. it appeared allarmed at my dog which was probably the cause of it's so readily attatching itself to me.

Meriwether Lewis
April 22, 1805

FIVE

BEAVER

You wouldn't think a beaver would be much of a threat to a big dog like me. But of all the animals I encountered during our journey, it was a beaver that nearly killed me.

It happened on a breezy day. The sails were up, and we were moving along. I was sitting next to Lewis in one of the boats. Sacagawea, the Indian woman who was traveling with us, was right behind me. Her arm rested on my back. My eyes were closed, but my nose was high in the air. I was taking in the smells, most of which were familiar. Suddenly the scent of beaver filled my nostrils.

Beavers were not new to me. During the first part of our trip, I loved chasing them out of their homes. On this particular day I was a bit tired, so I barely opened my eyes. I spotted them immediately. They were scurrying back and forth, working on a dam. Right away I noticed something different about these beavers—their size. They were the largest beavers I had ever seen, and I had seen a lot of beavers.

I barked to alert Lewis and the others. I figured they might want to stop. Beaver pelts were valuable trading, and the tails were a delicacy among the men. Also, there was one particularly large beaver, and I thought it would be fun to get him.

Lewis scanned the banks.

"Beavers," he called, pointing to the shore.

"Look at that big one," John Ordway exclaimed from the other end of the boat. He was one of the three sergeants.

"I want that one's tail, Captain," Drouillard said.

"Take him," Lewis said.

The men lowered the sail. Drouillard lifted his long rifle into position.

"Get ready, Seaman," Lewis said.

I was ready. I knew exactly what to do. I had done it a hundred times. I leaned forward.

"That's the biggest beaver yet, Captain," Ordway exclaimed.

Sacagawea placed her hand on my shoulder. She pulled back slightly.

Drouillard took aim. He was the best shot in the group, so I knew he'd make the kill. I felt a twinge of excitement. I would be retrieving the biggest beaver I had seen so far. I waited patiently.

Boom! The long rifle blasted the lead ball toward its target. The large beaver jerked backward.

"Got him!" Ordway yelled.

"He's still movin'," Lewis said.

The beaver half dove and half fell into the water.

Drouillard mumbled something in French.

"There he goes," Ordway said, pointing.

He didn't need to tell me. My eyes had not left that beaver. I waited for Lewis.

"Go get him," Lewis said.

I leaped into the river with my paws in motion. I felt especially strong as my paws propelled me through the water. The beaver saw me coming and changed direction. He was wounded, but his back webbed feet still made him a powerful swimmer.

I came up behind him and snapped at his tail. I missed.

I lunged for his neck. With a swish of his tail he turned. I missed again. This wasn't going to be as easy as I thought.

The beaver was facing the other way now, swimming hard, but not fast. I snapped at his tail. He twisted. I missed. He spun around and snapped at my back legs. I felt a sharp stab of pain. Then nothing.

Lewis whistled for me.

I tried to swim back to the boat, but it was difficult. My leg wasn't working right. Lewis and the men rowed toward me. It was a good thing, because suddenly I felt tired.

By the time they arrived, I was panting and not making much headway at all. Lewis and Sacagawea pulled me into the boat. I lay on the bottom, not moving. It was more than fatigue. I felt dizzy and all tingly inside. Sacagawea leaned down and stroked my neck. She whispered her native Shoshone language in my ear.

The next thing I knew, I was on shore, and Lewis was doing something to my leg.

"He cut an artery," I heard him say. His voice was low and filled with concern.

I closed my eyes.

I have seen life begin. I have seen life end. I had never thought much about it before. I had certainly never thought about my own life beginning or ending. Looking back on it, I think I was probably close to the end. At the time I didn't think about that. I wasn't worried. Lewis took care of everyone in our group. He would take care of me.

———

As I recovered, Sacagawea and Lewis cared for me. The men brought me lots of good meat: buffalo, deer, antelope. Lewis gave me a deer bone. I chewed it and sucked out all the delicious marrow.

It was two days before I looked at my leg. There was a cut across the upper part, not quite as long as I had thought it might be. There were stitches all along the cut. It is amazing what those long, sharp beaver teeth can do.

Now I see young dogs chase beavers. Those dogs bark and run. They don't respect the beaver. They'll learn.

———————

. . . one of the party wounded a beaver, and my dog as usual swam in to catch it; the beaver bit him through the hind leg and cut the artery; it was with great difficulty that I could stop the blood; I fear it will yet prove fatal to him.

Meriwether Lewis
May 19, 1805

SIX

BUFFALO

Buffalo!

When I hear the word, the hair on my neck stands up. I am filled with both excitement and fear. Buffaloes can be very peaceful animals, even shy, but when they stampede, they are as deadly as any creature I've seen. Once, I saw a buffalo trample trees like they were grass.

Not too long after my encounter with that over-sized beaver, I came head-to-head with a buffalo. It started out as a great evening. Pierre Cruzatte, one of the privates, played his fiddle. The men sang and stomped their feet and shouted around the campfire. Everyone was enjoying the fun.

Then, one by one, the men began to turn in. Pretty soon everyone was asleep except the sentinel and me. Many nights I stayed up with the sentinel. Men don't smell too well, so I keep my nose alert for any animals that might be prowling around the camp, especially bears and wildcats.

This particular night I strolled around the edge of the camp one last time. The men were sleeping, and there were several campfires going. Everything seemed in order. A raccoon or maybe an opossum wandered nearby, but that was not unusual.

I lay down in front of the captains' tent and rested my head on my paws. I listened to the night sounds, mostly crickets and owls—nothing worth getting up for. I closed my eyes, leaving my nose and ears to stay alert.

I heard it before I smelled it.

A splash in the water. Something swimming our way.

I waited and listened. More splashing.

This was a large, clumsy swimmer, definitely not a beaver. Maybe an antelope.

I lifted my head.

More splashing. Closer.

Getting out of the water. Stepping on our canoes. Definitely a big animal.

Then I smelled it. Buffalo.

This was a lone buffalo by the water's edge.

The sentry was not far from me. He heard it, too.

I stood and surveyed the campsite again. The captains' tent was surrounded by sleeping men.

I felt the ground vibrate. The buffalo was rampaging in our direction.

The sentry stood now. We were both looking toward the water. It was one of those moments when time stands still.

Suddenly, the buffalo appeared on the edge of the camp, charging directly toward a group of sleeping men. The sentry jumped into action. He waved his arms, screamed, and tried to scare the buffalo away. I barked.

The buffalo trampled one of the fires, then he turned and thundered past the group of sleeping men, barely missing their heads.

Our moment of relief was replaced with true horror. The buffalo was now headed straight for the captains' tent.

The sentry yelled again, but he was behind the buffalo. His yells made no difference. It was up to me. If I didn't stop the buffalo, the men sleeping in front of the tent would be trampled and Lewis and the others inside the tent would be crushed.

I jumped in front of the men and barked as I had never barked before. I barked, growled, and hissed all in a matter of seconds. The buffalo's black eyes were intense. He didn't stop.

I barked again, this time jumping onto my back paws and thrashing the air with my large front paws. If ever I wanted to be bear-dog, it was now. A flash of confusion crossed the buffalo's face. He swerved to the right and ran out of the camp. He missed the men just by inches.

The men jumped up and grabbed their guns. They took aim at anything and everything around them, but the buffalo was gone.

When the excitement died down, Lewis joined me at the campfire. He bent down and scratched my neck.

I knew what he was going to say before he said it. "Good job, Seaman."

———————

Last night we were all allarmed by a large buffaloe Bull, which swam over from the opposite shore . . . he then alarmed ran up the bank in full speed directly towards the fires, and was within 18 inches of the heads of some of the men who lay sleeping before the centinel could allarm him or make him change his course, still more alarmed, he now took his direction immediately towards our lodge. . . . my dog saved us by causing him to change his course a second time, which he did by turning a little to the right, and was quickly out of sight, leaving us by this time all in an uproar with our guns in or hands. . . .

Meriwether Lewis
May 29, 1805

SEVEN

KIDNAPPED

York and I were a double show. Indians would come to camp just to see us. York was black, like me. The Indians had never seen a black man before. They would rub York's skin to see if the color was painted on. They liked his curly hair, too. They thought he was somehow magical. York loved it. He would dance around and act crazy, as though he really did have great magic.

The Indians were just as interested in me. Lewis let me do tricks. Some Indians thought I was a mini-ature bear that Lewis had tamed. Others realized I was a dog. Most thought I had great magic. I have to admit that York and I were pretty convincing.

I got along well with the Indians, especially the Mandans, the Shoshones, and the Nez Percé. They were friendly and helped us a lot. The Clatsop Indians were different. My men didn't seem to like them too much. I could tell by the way they acted when we were in Clatsop territory. Their bodies were stiff, and their heads were raised slightly. Their voices sounded tense.

The Clatsop Indians would come around the camp, and then next thing I knew, the men were hollering about something missing. It seems the Clatsops were stealing our things. Lewis posted double guards around the camp and the boats.

Most of the time the men did not try to get back the things the Indians took. Lewis said it wasn't worth starting an Indian fight over. Then one day, the Indians stole something that was worth fighting over. They stole a member of our party. Me!

I was outside the camp sniffing after a squirrel when the first Indian appeared. I smelled him before I saw him, but I didn't think anything of it.

The Indian came closer. He spoke in a friendly voice. Then I noticed two more. They moved like dark shadows, blending in with the trees. Even that didn't make me suspicious. Indians would often sneak around, hunting some prey.

I guess they weren't hunting prey because they came over to me. The first Indian scratched my neck. He spoke softly. I had no idea what he was saying.

The second Indian stepped forward. I thought he was going to scratch me, too, but instead he slipped a rope around my neck. I jerked my head. I had not had a rope since my days on the dock. I glared at that Indian. I jerked my head again. The rope pulled tighter.

The third Indian dipped his hand into his pouch and pulled out a piece of meat.

Beaver! I love beaver. I stepped forward and took the meat. I swallowed it in one bite. It was delicious. I seemed to have grown more fond of beaver since my leg was cut.

The Indians tugged on the rope and beckoned me to come. Something about this wasn't right. I stood fast.

Another piece of beaver.

I went.

I trotted along behind the Indians. They were moving a little faster than I wanted, but I was used to Lewis's fast pace, so it wasn't a problem.

Some noise grew behind us. I couldn't tell exactly what it was.

The Indians stopped and crouched down around me. I felt the same tension in their bodies that I felt in my men when the bears growl at night. The Indians whispered nervously. This should have alerted me that they were up to no good, but the third Indian was right beside me, and the smell of beaver was strong from his pouch.

More noise behind us. Voices. Familiar.

The Indians ran. The rope pulled tighter, which I didn't like, but I followed. I turned my ears to hear what was behind us that was upsetting the Indians.

Men's voices. My men's voices. They sounded upset.

Then I realized: These Indians were taking me, and my men didn't like it.

I stopped immediately. The rope jerked out of the Indian's hand.

He turned and looked surprised. He picked up the rope and pulled. I didn't budge. He yelled to his friends. One of them grabbed the rope. Together they pulled. I stood my ground.

More yelling came from my men, who were getting closer.

The Indians gave a final tug. Nothing.

The Indians stared at me. I stared back.

They quickly dropped the rope and ran.

Good-bye, Indians. Good-bye, beaver.

My men were glad to see me.

They scratched me. They hugged me. All the way back to the camp they grumbled about the Clatsops.

Lewis was especially glad to see me. It was almost as though he thought I wasn't coming back. Lewis didn't need to worry. Those Clatsop Indians were sneaky, but not sneaky enough to separate us.

———————

. . . three of this same tribe of villains
. . . stole my dog this evening, and took
him towards their village; I was shortly

afterwards informed of this . . . and sent three men in pursuit of the theives with orders if they made the least resistence or difficulty in surrendering the dog to fire on them; they overtook these fellows or reather came within sight of them . . . the indians discovering the party in pursuit of them left the dog and fled.

Meriwether Lewis
April 11, 1806

EIGHT

DEER

I loved to hunt. We all did. And the more we hunted, the better we worked as a team—Lewis and I and the men. We each knew what the others could do, and no one hesitated when it came to doing the job. One of my favorite hunts occurred on a cold May morning on our way back east.

We were camped by the river. It had been an especially cold night, and Lewis and I were up early, sitting by the fire. I loved to sit by the fire with Lewis. Sometimes he would talk about what he was thinking or what he wanted to accomplish that day. This morning he was quiet.

A couple of young Indians had spent the night with us. They were at the fire, too. We were warming ourselves when Sergeant Nathaniel Pryor walked by and left camp. He had his gun with him, and I figured he was going out to hunt. Outside camp there was a salt deposit, which the deer liked to come to and lick. Pryor was headed in that direction. He was one of the best hunters in our group, and in the past couple of days he had gotten several deer.

The Indians and Lewis and I stayed by the fire.

A few minutes later we heard the shot.

Sergeant Pryor yelled, "Captain, your way!"

Lewis and I jumped up as one. We started for the lick. We could see the deer running toward us. I was amazed at his size. He was almost twice as big as the other deer in this area. He was limping slightly, favoring his right side.

"Toward the river!" Lewis yelled at me.

I had been thinking the same thing and had already changed my direction. I was circling around the deer to force him to the river. That's where we would have the best chance to get him. Swimming would slow him down, and he would be an easy target.

The deer saw me. It startled him. He stumbled back and turned right. I darted left. He obliged me by turning back to the left, toward the river.

"Good, Seaman!" I heard Lewis yell.

I heard the sound of horses, the horses that belonged to the two Indians. I could tell from the rumbling ground that they were galloping toward the river. I figured Sergeant Pryor was on his way to the river as well.

The deer reached the river. He paused for a moment, as if contemplating his options. He didn't have many. He looked back, saw me bounding toward him, and, without another thought, he jumped into the river. He swam hard, straight across. His injury didn't seem to slow him down much, but he was breathing heavily.

The Indians were in the river now, too, on horseback, racing for the opposite side. The deer was almost to the riverbank. The Indians reached

the bank first. They split up and approached the deer from two directions. When the deer saw the Indians, he jumped back into the river and started swimming back toward us.

Lewis had caught up with me. From the bank we admired the skill of the Indians and their horses.

"Got him covered, Captain!" Sergeant Pryor yelled from a few yards downriver. He was a good shot, and the deer was well within his range.

When the deer reached the bank, Sergeant Pryor took aim and fired. The deer fell, and I felt the thud under my feet as he hit the ground.

The Indians swam back across the river on their horses and helped pull the deer away from the bank.

Lewis gave half the deer to the Indians. That was like Lewis.

As we sat around the campfire that night, the men talked about the chase and the part each of us had played. When they talked about me, Lewis put his hand on my head. I closed my eyes and enjoyed the moment.

Sergt. Pryor wounded a deer early this morning in a lick near camp; my dog pursud it into the river; the two young Indian men who had remained with us all night mounted their horses swam the river and drove the deer into the water again; Sergt. Pryor killed it as it reached the shore on this side, the indians returned as they had passed over. we directed half this deer to be given to the indians, . . .

Meriwether Lewis
May 23, 1806

NINE

MY FAVORITE WORDS

I've seen dogs with good men. And dogs with men who are just plain mean. Most dogs hope for a man they can understand. It's great when you know what you're supposed to do. Lewis knew exactly what I could do, and he let me do it. In fact, it got so that Lewis didn't have to tell me what he wanted me to do. I knew.

Lewis would shoot an antelope, or some animal, and I'd wait. We'd watch it fall. Then Lewis would reload his gun. That's when I'd retrieve the prey. Lewis didn't have to say a word. I knew what to do and when to do it.

Some men talk all the time, even when they're not telling you what to do. Not Lewis. Lewis and I would walk to the top of a mountain and just stand there, him looking out over the view, and me with my nose high in the air. We didn't say a word. We didn't have to.

For Lewis and me, it was more than just understanding each other. We suited each other perfectly. Only a few dogs are lucky enough to have a man who suits them like that. I've thought about that, why Lewis and I were so well suited. I'm not sure I know exactly.

Lewis was a great man. I know that. The men knew it, too. They would do anything for Lewis. They loved him, especially Clark. I think Clark loved Lewis about as much as I did. I never heard Lewis or Clark say a harsh word to each other. And it was more than just getting along. They fit together, too. Of course that was different. They were both men. Dog and man can fit together like no others do. Lewis and I had that fit. By the end of our journey, we were as close as an animal and its hide.

How did we get that close? I think the wilderness had something to do with it. Lewis and I would have been close anywhere, but the wilderness brought out the best in both of us. We were made for that territory.

I was made for it in every way: my size, my fur, my paws, my instincts. I love running, hunting, swimming, and retrieving. I was happiest when I was doing those things.

Lewis was happiest in the wilderness, too. Sometimes I think Lewis preferred the wilderness to people. He would spend hours looking at plants, examining animal specimens, and measuring the sky. He and I spent a lot of time hiking and exploring. We loved the stimulation of the wilderness. It was perfect for both of us.

No dog could have a more perfect life than I had. My dreams let me relive it over and over. They fill me with what I saw and what I did. I dream of . . .

Bears prowling around at night, keeping me awake.

Lewis and I, overlooking the Pacific Ocean, smelling the salt air.

Prickly pear cactus needles stuck in my paws, and Lewis tenderly pulling them out one by one.

And that triumphal return to St. Louis. Men, women, and children running to the docks to meet us. Dogs barking. Horses in an uproar. People shouting and cheering.

I look at Lewis. He looks at me. He's smiling. He places his hand on my head. I push my head further into his hand. Then he says my favorite words.

"Good job, Seaman."

. . . my dog was of the newfoundland breed very active strong and docile . . .

Meriwether Lewis
September 11, 1803

AFTERWORD

Where Meriwether Lewis purchased Seaman is a mystery. Newfoundlands were popular along the East Coast, so two likely places are Washington, D.C., where Lewis lived and worked as Thomas Jefferson's secretary, and Philadelphia, where he went to prepare for the expedition. Another possibility is Pittsburgh, where Lewis actually began the journey. Seaman is first mentioned in Lewis's journal on September 11, 1803, as they sailed on the Ohio River from Pittsburgh to St. Louis.

For years writers called Lewis's dog Scannon. This was not questioned until 1984, when Donald

Jackson, a great Lewis and Clark scholar, was doing research about the rivers, streams, and creeks that Lewis and Clark had named. Every name had a meaning, but Jackson could not figure out "Seaman's Creek" in Montana. He went back to the original drawings and writings and discovered that in Scannon, the *c* was actually an *e* and the *nn* was an *m*, thus "Scannon" was actually *Seaman*. Seaman's Creek, now called Monture Creek, still exists in Montana.

The last time Seaman is mentioned in a journal is July 15, 1806, in Montana when Lewis wrote:

> . . . the musquetoes continue to infest us in such manner that we can scarcely exist; . . . my dog even howls with the torture he experiences from them, . . .

The expedition arrived back in St. Louis two months later, September 23, 1806. Although most scholars believed Seaman completed the journey (his death or loss would surely have been mentioned in one of the many journals), no one knew for certain until recently, when another Lewis and Clark scholar, Jim Holmberg, discovered a book written in 1814, which listed epitaphs and inscriptions. The book lists an inscription on a dog collar (most likely destroyed in a fire in 1817) in a museum in Virginia. The inscription reads:

> The greatest traveller of my species. My name is SEAMAN, the dog of captain Meriwether Lewis, whom I accompanied to the Pacifick ocean through the interior of the continent of North America.

A note under the inscription goes on to say of Seaman that when Meriwether Lewis died in 1809

> no gentle means could draw him from the spot of interment. He refused to take every kind of food, which was offered him, and actually pined away and died with grief upon his master's grave!

Sources

Introduction and Afterword

Ambrose, Stephen. *Undaunted Courage* (New York: Simon & Schuster, 1996).

Holmberg, James J. "Seaman's Fate?" *We Proceeded On* 26, no. 1 (February 2000).

Jackson, Donald, and Ernest S. Osgood. *The Lewis and Clark Expedition's Newfoundland Dog* (Great Falls, Montana: WPO Publication No. 12, Lewis and Clark Trail Heritage Foundation, Inc., July 1997).

Journal Entries

All quotes from Meriwether Lewis are from *The Journals of the Lewis and Clark Expedition*, edited by Gary E. Moulton, 13 volumes (Lincoln: University of Nebraska Press, 1983–2000), and are used with permission of the publisher.